This
Harry
book belongs to

....

SCELIDOSAURUS
(ske-LI-doh-SAW-rus)

TYRANNOSAURUS
(tie-RAN-oh-SAW-rus)

TRICERATOPS
(try-SER-a-tops)

STEGOSAURUS
(STEG-oh-SAW-rus)

PTERODACTYL
(TER-oh-DAC-til)

APATOSAURUS
(a-PAT-oh-SAW-rus)

ANCHISAURUS
(AN-ki-SAW-rus)

SCELIDOSAURUS
(ske-LI-doh-SAW-rus)

TYRANNOSAURUS
(tie-RAN-oh-SAW-rus)

TRICERATOPS
(try-SER-a-tops)

STEGOSAURUS
(STEG-oh-SAW-rus)

PTERODACTYL
(TER-oh-DAC-til)

APATOSAURUS
(a-PAT-oh-SAW-rus)

ANCHISAURUS
(AN-ki-SAW-rus)

For Rita Evans, Ella Rose Kennedy and Teddy Traynor

This book is dedicated with admiration and affection to Louis Burnard,
the son part of Bopsom and Son, High Street, Kington, Herefordshire, England.

It was Louis who, aged seven, told his mum and dad that he might be little but
he was determined to make a difference for endangered animals. It was he who made
the exquisite drawings for a series of "Arkworks" greetings cards that have since
sold in thousands for the benefit of animal conservation.

It was Louis's determination, imagination and energy that inspired this story.

PUFFIN BOOKS

Published by the Penguin Group: London, New York, Ireland, Australia, Canada, India, New Zealand and South Africa
Penguin Books Ltd, Registered Offices: 80 Strand, London WC2R 0RL, England

www.penguin.com

First published 2005
Published in this edition 2006
5 7 9 10 8 6 4

Text copyright © Ian Whybrow, 2005
Illustrations copyright © Adrian Reynolds, 2005
All rights reserved

The moral right of the author and illustrator has been asserted

Set in Goudy
Manufactured in China

ISBN-13: 978–0–14150–004–1
ISBN-10: 0–14150–004–2

Harry and the Dinosaurs Go Wild

Ian Whybrow and Adrian Reynolds

PUFFIN

It was a long drive to the safari park but it was worth it.
Apatosaurus saw an animal just like Triceratops.
"That's a rhinoceros," said Harry.
"Triceratops has got more horns."

Mum liked the giraffes best and Nan
liked the zebras.
  The monkeys were funny but the
man said not to feed them.

Sam asked him if they had pandas but the man
said no, they were endangered animals.
Harry wanted to know what endangered meant.
Sam said he was too little to understand.

Nan helped. She bought Harry a book about endangered animals. She thought it was sad about the Sumatran tigers. People kept hunting them so there were only a few left in the whole world.

Harry really wanted to help but he had no money.
"I want to save some animals," he said.
"What can I do, Mum?"

Sam said, "Tuh! What a waste of time!"
  She said he was miles too small to make any
difference. That's why Harry made her do a smudge
with her lipstick.

Mum took Harry off to settle down.
Then they looked on the Internet
and found lots of endangered animals.

Mum said why not do a poster? Harry could put it up in his window. Then maybe other people would help the animals too.

Harry liked that idea. He got out his drawing stuff straight away. Trouble was, it was hard to know which animal to save first.

The dinosaurs said, "Raaaah! We want to save some BIG animals!"

So they started drawing.

   Tyrannosaurus did a polar bear.

   Pterodactyl asked Harry to help him do a gorilla.

   "Wait till I've finished my blue whale," said Harry.
"Blue whales are bigger than trains, bigger than
dinosaurs, bigger than thirty-two elephants!"

Stegosaurus did an army tank.
"Army tanks don't need saving!" said Triceratops.
"Do a tree frog instead."

Mum said the drawings were excellent.
She helped put the words on.
LET'S SAVE THESE ENDANGERED ANIMALS!

Nan said, "Why not talk to Mr Bopsom?
He might put up a poster in his shop window!
Then people can see the pictures when they go shopping!"

Mr Bopsom loved the pictures but he thought they might
be a bit too small for a poster.
He asked Harry if he could draw them bigger.
Harry said no, sorry, his pictures always came out small.

"That's a shame," said Mr Bopsom. "Because saving animals is important!"

Poor Harry. He went home feeling maybe Sam was right. Maybe you had to be big before you could be any use.

The very next day, Mr Bopsom was on the phone.
"I've had an idea!" he said. "Can you do me *lots* more pictures?"

So Harry and the dinosaurs did more birds
and bugs and reptiles
and *lots more dinosaurs!*

Then off they went to give them to Mr Bopsom.

When Harry went into the shop two weeks later
he was amazed! Mr Bopsom had made all the
drawings into cards.
   He said that every time somebody bought a card,
some of the money went to save endangered animals.

Everybody loved them. They said, "Marvellous!"
"What a brilliant idea!"
"So original!"
"Four cards for me, please!"

The lady from the paper came and was very impressed.
  "What a wonderful thing you've done!" she said.
  "Raahh!" said Apatosaurus. "Save the strawberry
poison arrow frog!"
  "Raahh!" said Pterodactyl. "Save the teeny
blue tongued skink!"

And Harry said, "Quite right, my dinosaurs! Because even
if you are as tiny as a tick on the tail of a green turtle,
you can still do something that makes a BIG difference!"

ENDOSAURUS

SCELIDOSAURUS
(ske-LI-doh-SAW-rus)

TYRANNOSAURUS
(tie-RAN-oh-SAW-rus)

TRICERATOPS
(try-SER-a-tops)

STEGOSAURUS
(STEG-oh-SAW-rus)

PTERODACTYL
(TER-oh-DAC-til)

APATOSAURUS
(a-PAT-oh-SAW-rus)

ANCHISAURUS
(AN-ki-SAW-rus)

SCELIDOSAURUS
(ske-LI-doh-SAW-rus)

TYRANNOSAURUS
(tie-RAN-oh-SAW-rus)

TRICERATOPS
(try-SER-a-tops)

STEGOSAURUS
(STEG-oh-SAW-rus)

PTERODACTYL
(TER-oh-DAC-til)

APATOSAURUS
(a-PAT-oh-SAW-rus)

ANCHISAURUS
(AN-ki-SAW-rus)

Look out for all of Harry's adventures!

Harry and the Bucketful of Dinosaurs

Harry finds some old, plastic dinosaurs and cleans them, finds out their names and takes them everywhere with him – until, one day, they get lost… Will he ever find them?

ISBN 0140569804

Harry and the Snow King

There's just enough snow for Harry to build a very small snow king. But then the snow king disappears – who's kidnapped him?

ISBN 0140569863

Harry and the Robots

Harry's robot is sent to the toy hospital to be fixed, so Harry and Nan decide to make a new one. When Nan has to go to hospital, Harry knows just how to help her get better!

ISBN 0140569820

Harry and the Dinosaurs say "Raahh!"

Harry's dinosaurs are acting strangely. They're hiding all over the house, refusing to come out… Could it be because today is the day of Harry's dentist appointment?

ISBN 0140569812

Harry and the Dinosaurs Romp in the Swamp

Harry has to play at Charlie's house and doesn't want to share his dinosaurs. But when Charlie builds a fantastic swamp, Harry and the dinosaurs can't help but join in the fun!

ISBN 0140569847

Harry and the Dinosaurs make a Christmas Wish

Harry and the dinosaurs would *love* to own a duckling. They wait till Christmas and make a special wish, but Santa leaves them something even more exciting…!

ISBN 0141380179 (hbk)
ISBN 0140569529 (pbk)

ISBN 0140569839

ISBN 0140569855

Harry and the Dinosaurs play Hide-and-Seek
Harry and the Dinosaurs have a Very Busy Day

Join in with Harry and his dinosaurs for some peep-through fold-out fun! These exciting books about shapes and colours make learning easy!